THIMBLE
WONGA BONKERS

Jon Blake lives in Cardiff with his partner and two young children. He qualified as a teacher in 1979. His first story was published in 1984; since then he has earned his living as a writer of books, TV and radio scripts, and as a teacher of creative writing. Previous books include the bestselling *You're a Hero Daley B, Stinky Fingers' House of Fun* and *The Last Free Cat*. His first Thimble book, *Thimble Monkey Superstar,* was published in 2016. It was selected for the Summer Reading Challenge and shortlisted for the Lollies 2017 Laugh out Loud Book Awards. The second book, *Thimble Holiday Havoc*, was published in 2017.

Martin Chatterton's own books include *Monster and Chips* (OUP) and some of the *Middle School* books with James Patterson, and he has illustrated many, many books in the UK and Australia, including stories by Julia Donaldson and Tony Bradman.

THIMBLE
WONGA BONKERS

JON BLAKE

Firefly

**ILLUSTRATED BY
MARTIN CHATTERTON**

First published in 2020
by Firefly Press
25 Gabalfa Road, Llandaff North,
Cardiff, CF14 2JJ
www.fireflypress.co.uk

Text © Jon Blake 2020
Illustrations © Martin Chatterton 2020

A CIP catalogue record of this book
is available from the British Library.

ISBN 978-1-913102-10-4
ebook ISBN 978-1-913102-11-1

*This book has been published with the support
of the Welsh Books Council.*

Design by: Claire Brisley
Printed and bound by: PULSIO SARL

CONTENTS

CHAPTER ONE

THE SOUND OF PACKING BAGS AND DAD DREAMS OF COWS

It was a dark day in Dawson Castle, our little bungalow home. Dad paced the floor of the Great Hall. I chewed hard on my last long fingernail. Thimble, our monkey, covered his head with a pillow. I hadn't told my furry friend what was about to happen, but he could sense it was something bad.

From Mum's room, meanwhile, there came a sinister sound.

The sound of bags being packed.

'You're sure you're going to do this?' Dad asked.

'Quite sure, thank you, Douglas.'

'You're not worried what effect it will have on Jams?'

'Jams will be fine.'

'Or Thimble?'

'Thimble will be fine.'

'Or me?'

'Douglas, you're a grown man. You can cope with me being away for a week.'

The conversation ended, just as it had done the time before, and the time before that. In fact, Mum and Dad had had this conversation thirteen times, ever since Mum first said she was going away for a spa week with her friends. That's a week of having your hands and feet tweaked and your head rubbed. A silly fad, according to Dad, probably invented by the Americans.

Half an hour later, Mum stood in the Great Hall (what normal people call the lounge) and prepared to say her goodbyes.

'Now, remember,' she said. 'I don't want you to ring me unless it's an emergency. The aim of this week is to relax.'

'It's already an emergency,' said Dad.

'Oh nonsense,' said Mum.

'But ... there's hardly any food! What will we eat?'

'For goodness sake, Douglas, you know how to shop, don't you?'

'I need money to shop,' mumbled Dad.

Mum fished in her bag. 'Here's thirty quid

to be going on with,' she said. 'If you need any more, the petty-cash box is on my desk.'

'Now I feel like you're giving me pocket money,' said Dad.

'OK,' said Mum, 'I'll give it to Jams.'

'What?' stammered Dad.

'Now I can get *Footy Weekly*!' I cried.

'On second thoughts,' said Mum, 'I'll give it to Thimble.'

'What?' said Dad.

'Here, Thimble.'

Thimble lolloped over and Mum tucked the money into his shirt pocket.

'I don't believe this!' said Dad.

'I often get Thimble to carry my money,' said Mum. 'He's very responsible.'

'Responsible for driving me mad,' said Dad.

'Just trust him. He's not stupid. Are you, Thimble?'

Thimble nodded eagerly, then blew a
raspberry at Dad.

'Did you see that?'

'Relax, Douglas,' said Mum. 'He's just
being playful.'

'I will relax when you come back from
this infernal spa week!'.

As if on cue, the doorbell rang, and in came Diz, Roz, Shaz, Jo, Ree, Mags and Tigerlily. Mum double-kissed them all in the continental style, then there was lavish praise for her new walking boots and much fuss for Thimble and me. Meanwhile, Dad shrank into a chair, hugging himself as if this would protect him from the roomful of loud and excited women.

'Cheer up, Douglas!' said Diz. 'May never happen!'

'It is happening,' mumbled Dad.

'Are you sure you don't want to come with us? I don't know how we'll cope without a man.'

'Oh,' said Dad. 'Err ... what about Jams?'

There was a moment's silence, then suddenly the room was full of raucous laughter.

'I didn't think you'd take me seriously!' said Diz.

'Look at his face, poor love,' said Shaz.

'Sorry, Doug,' said Diz.

'Douglas,' muttered Dad.

'Right,' said Mum. 'I shall love you and leave you.'

'The first would be a nice change,' said Dad.

Mum gave me an enormous hug, followed by a peck on the cheek for Dad and a little squeeze for Thimble, which turned into a rather long squeeze, as it was difficult to prise Thimble's arms from around her neck. Finally, however, Mum broke free, and the noisy crowd of friends bustled out of the door, leaving Dawson Castle rather quiet and sad.

'I don't like that Diz,' said Dad. 'Diz: what's that short for anyway?'

'I like her,' I said.

'You're a clever boy,' said Dad, 'but a poor judge of character. Right, let's make a shopping list and go to the shops. And, oh, just slip your shirt off, Thimble, and I'll run the iron over it.'

Thimble's hand shot to his shirt pocket, which he covered with grim resolve. Just as Mum had said, he wasn't stupid.

'Right,' said Dad. 'Lets start off with the essentials. Number one, biscuits.'

'Biscuits?' I replied. 'Shouldn't that be bread, or milk?'

'I was just coming to those,' said Dad. 'Biscuits ... bread ... milk ... taters...'

'Say potatoes, Dad. Slang confuses Thimble.'

'Thimble won't be putting things in the trolley,' said Dad, 'or going anywhere near it.'

'Can't he push it?'

'Hmm. Actually, that's quite a good idea. It'll keep his hands off everything else.'

'Brilliant! Did you hear that, Thimble? You're pushing the trolley!'

Thimble was overjoyed, and just to show how well he would perform this task, he pushed my walker all the way to the supermarket. For those who don't know me, a walker is a frame on wheels which I use because my legs are a bit wonky. I can walk without my walker, except sometimes my left foot catches on my right and I go flying over and people rush up going *Is he alright?* and Dad goes *He's fine, he's fine* and I go *Ow!* and Thimble just gets hold of me and yanks me to my feet. Thimble has amazingly strong arms.

Today, thankfully, I didn't fall over, and no one took much notice of me in the supermarket. Thimble, on the other hand, had every pair of eyes on him, which irritated Dad no end.

'What's the matter?' he grumbled. 'Never seen a monkey pushing a trolley before? Why don't you take a picture? No, not really!'

The nosy customers were quickly

forgotten, however, as soon as we reached the biscuit shelves.

'Stand back, Jams,' said Dad. 'This is my territory.'

Dad's eyes went left-right, left-right across the shelves like a cat after a fly.

'Can we have Jammie Dodgers?' I asked.

'Too jammy,' replied Dad.

'Fig rolls?'

'Too figgy.'

'Marshmallows?'

'Too marshy. Ah! Here we are. Malted milks.'

'Not malted milks, Dad! They taste like sick!'

'But they've got a little cow on them.'

'And?'

'And it's rather reassuring.'

'I don't find it reassuring.'

'You will when you're older.'

'How depressing.'

'The detail's marvellous, Jams. If you look closely, you'll notice a little gate behind the little cow.'

'Can we just have a vote on it, Dad?' I suggested.

'What's the point? I'll vote for and you'll vote against.'

'Thimble can vote too.'

Dad snapped out of his dream of cows and gates and happy days long ago which never really existed.

'Where is Thimble?' he asked.

'He was right here a second ago,' I replied.

'Well, he's not here now! Quick, find him before he does something crazy!'

I went one way, Dad the other. No sign of him by the breakfast cereals. No sign of him by the petfoods .. Yikes, where was he? Dad had no more success.

'I've done aisles one to four,' he said. 'What about you?'

'Aisles five to eight. That's all of them.'

'Did you look in the freezers?'

'He couldn't get a trolley in the freezers.'

'Then where the blazes is he?

'Search me, Dad. We've looked everywhere except…'

'What?'

'Dad, I've just seen something.'

'What?'

'Promise you won't go mad?'

'What?'

'Thimble's at the checkout.'

'NO-O-O-O-O-O-O-O-O-O-O!'

As usual I was faster than Dad, even with my walker. But not fast enough.

'Thimble!' I cried. 'What have you done?'

Thimble reached into his pocket and drew out a till receipt and 60p change, which he proudly offered up to me. Behind him was our trolley, packed to the brim with bananas.

CHAPTER TWO
SOOTHING RAINDROPS AND A WHOLE LOAD OF FIREWOOD

'Ninety-six ... ninety-seven ... ninety-eight,'
I counted. 'That's it, Dad, ninety-eight.'

Dad's head sank to the refectory table.

'Ninety-eight bananas!' he wailed. 'What
are we going to do with ninety-eight
bananas?'

'Banana fritters?' I suggested.

'Banana fritters? Are you joking? To make
fritters you need flour! Bicarb! Oil! All
we've got is flipping bananas!'

I sighed. 'Haven't you got *any* money
anywhere, Dad?'

'No, Jams, I have not. I'm a writer,
remember. I would have to get a book

published to get money, and no one wants
to publish my books, apart from…'

Dad mysteriously shut up.

'Apart from who?'

'Never mind.'

'Someone wants to publish your books?
Why aren't you sending them your books?'

'They want something from me,' said Dad.
'Something I'm not prepared to give.'

'Dad, explain yourself! *What* don't you

want to give them?'

'End of conversation.'

'Oh, come on, Dad. You can't just leave me in suspense!'

'It's what authors do.' Dad ripped off three bananas, handed one to me, dropped one in front of Thimble, then began peeling one himself.

'Look,' I said. 'Thimble's peeling his from the other end to us. Isn't that interesting?'

'Fascinating,' said Dad.

'I wonder if all monkeys peel them from that end?'

'Maybe we should go to the zoo and find out,' said Dad, bitterly. 'Because that's where monkeys normally live.'

Dad said this sentence very slowly and deliberately, with his eyes fixed on Thimble, but Thimble wasn't in the least worried.

Thimble knew Dad would never take him back to a zoo, not after the last time (if you don't know about that you need to read *Thimble Monkey Superstar*).

'Another banana?' I offered.

'No thanks,' said Dad, grumpily. 'I'm going to chop wood.'

This was a sure sign Dad was getting stressed. As we had no fires, there really was no point in making firewood. So when Dad chopped wood, it was just to make himself feel better. Sometimes he'd chop for hours, finally coming in with icicles dangling from his nose and sores all over his hands. Usually I'd ask him how the chopping went, and most often he wouldn't even remember.

Today he only chopped for an hour or so. He was probably weak from the lack of food. When he came in, I was at the computer, bashing away at my latest novel.

'Where's Thimble?' he asked.

'Dunno,' I said.

'Have you heard him at all?'

'Come to think of it, he has been quiet.'

'That's always a bad sign.'

I called for Thimble. No answer.

'*Now* what's he up to?' said Dad.

He went to the kitchen, took one step inside, skidded up into the air and crashed on to his bum.

'Are you alright?' I said, hurrying to the rescue.

'A banana skin!' said Dad. He put his hand down to prise himself up, then that skidded away as well.

'Another banana skin!' he cried.

I viewed the scene before me. The kitchen

was carpeted from wall to wall with banana skins.

'Uh-oh,' I said.

'Tie everything down!' cried Dad. 'Thimble's on a sugar high!'

We knew the routine. Dad grabbed the vases and ornaments; I got the pictures off the walls. We'd just got the plant pots into the cupboards when the door burst open and Thimble flew down the room doing flik-flaks then back the other way bouncing on his bum. Hardly had he disappeared out of the door than he was back again, swinging across the ceiling by the chandeliers. We breathed a sigh of relief as he exited the house into the castle grounds (which normal people call the back yard), only to gasp in horror as he came dashing back with something very lethal in his monkey grip.

'Dad!' I cried. 'The axe!'

'What idiot left that out?' gasped Dad.

'Get it off him!'

'Too late.' Thimble was out of the West Door and on to the street.

'After him!' I cried, but Dad laid a hand on my arm.

'What's the point? There's no trees for miles so he can't do much harm. Let him

have a good run round so he comes back tired.'

I wasn't at all sure about this, but Thimble had been out in the street many times and always found his way home. So I sat back and tried to relax, while Dad put some music on the record player, which was what he called the stereo.

'Chopin's *Raindrops*,' he said. 'Blissfully soothing.'

Dad sank into his favourite chair, gazed wistfully at the ceiling and gently conducted the music with his little finger. 'Is there anything better for the soul,' he said, 'than the sound of...'

Suddenly Dad sat bolt upright. '*What was that*?' he said.

'What?'

'Something just fell past the window!'

'What did it look like?'

'Big! Tall! Dark!'

'You must be seeing things, Dad. Like you said, there's no trees for miles.'

'I am not seeing things!'

Dad rose from his chair and marched to the West Door, me following. Outside we were greeted by the sight of Thimble, jumping up and down in delight. At his feet was the awesome sight of a felled telegraph pole.

'Thimble!' cried Dad. 'What have you done?'

Thimble dropped the axe and made the sign for *firewood*.

'Quick, Jams! Get the bolt cutters!'

'What are we going to do?'

'Cut off the telephone lines so we can hide the darned thing!'

'But then people won't be able to use their phones.'

'Good! Then they won't be able to ring the police!'

I didn't bother to argue, even though, unlike Dad, I knew that almost everyone had a mobile. In fact, just as Dad started cutting the wires, I could see one of these mobiles in the hands of a man down the road in camo trousers.

'I think you're being filmed, Dad,' I said.

'Nosy parkers!' said Dad. 'Haven't they got anything better to do?'

'We can't take it into the house now,' I said.

'What else are we supposed to with it?'

'Put it in the recycling?'

'Be serious.'

'Maybe we should report it to the police,' I

suggested. 'If we report it, they won't think we did it.'

'We didn't do it,' said Dad. 'That thing did.' He pointed at Thimble, who was watching Dad with great curiosity.

'They'll never think a monkey did it,' I said.

Dad cut the last wire and sighed. 'OK. We'll take it down the police station. But leave all the talking to me.'

It wasn't easy transporting that telegraph pole. We propped one end up on my walker, guided by me, with Thimble in the middle and Dad at the other end. It was a monstrous weight and, by the time we reached the Dogsbridge Road, I was flagging.

'Can't we get the bus?' I suggested.

'Are you mad?' said Dad. 'How are we going to get a telegraph pole on a bus?'

'What about the long bendy ones? They have special spaces for wheelchairs and prams.'

'Jams, it's not a wheelchair. It's not a pram. It's a telegraph pole. They don't have special spaces for telegraph poles. Besides, we don't want to draw attention to ourselves.'

'Hate to say it, Dad, but we're already getting that.'

Dad gave a fierce stare to the gathering crowds of onlookers. 'What's the matter?' he said. 'Never seen a disabled boy and a monkey carrying a telegraph pole?'

'Why don't you take a picture?' I added.

'No, not really!' said Dad.

Thankfully, at last, we did reach the police

station, which was a lovely new building with automatic doors. (If you don't know what happened to the old police station, you can read about that in *Thimble Monkey Superstar*.) It was good that the doors opened automatically, otherwise the police might have thought they were being attacked with a battering ram. As it was they didn't even notice we'd come in. The desk sergeant and a PC were busy watching a computer screen and obviously enjoying whatever-it-was very much. The sergeant was laughing in a haw-haw funny donkey fashion while the PC kept up a soft, steady snigger.

'How rude,' whispered Dad, 'and how unprofessional.'

The two police officers continued haw-hawing, sniggering and generally ignoring us.

'Say something,' I said.

'A-hem!' said Dad. 'A-HEM!'

'Be with you in a moment,' said the sergeant, eyes still glued to the screen.

'Don't let us spoil your amusement,' said Dad.

'Can you believe that?' said the sergeant.

'I thought I'd seen everything in this job,' said the PC, 'but I've never seen a monkey chop down a telegraph pole before!'

A look of alarm came over Dad's face. He turned towards me with an urgent whisper. 'Jams!' he hissed. 'Start backing out of the door very, very quietly!'

This was easier said than done as my walker does not go backwards. We were as stuck as canned ham.

CHAPTER THREE

THEY USE MUSTARD ON DOGS AND HUMP-BACKED BRIDGES ON MONKEYS

It was a simple choice. Dad could pay an on-the-spot fine of £80 for criminal damage, or he could go to court. If he went to court he could end up paying twice as much and getting a criminal record. Through gritted teeth he agreed to pay the £80.

There was only one problem. Dad hadn't got £80. For that reason we were accompanied back to Dawson Castle by PC Wendy Bagshaw so that Dad could raid Mum's petty-cash box. PC Bagshaw was a woman of few words and even less sense of humour. She did not fall for my charms, nor Thimble's, and certainly not Dad's. She was

only interested in
the £80.

Dad, Thimble
and I crept into
Mum's bedchamber
(bedroom) where
the petty-cash
box lived. It was
almost as if we
were sneaking into

a shrine. The cash box was black and shiny
with a little silver key. It seemed to promise
all the secrets of the universe, as well as
a big wodge of notes and oodles of small
change.

'No one is to touch that key but me,' said
Dad.

'Don't say that,' I replied.

'Why not?'

'Thimble will want it now.'

Too late. Thimble was already on his way across the room. Dad did his best to beat him to the petty-cash box, but it was really no contest. In one unbroken movement, Thimble had snatched the key from the box and scuttered under Mum's desk to protect his booty.

'Thimble,' said Dad, 'give me the key.'

Thimble replied with a burst of excited monkey-chatter.

'Thimble,' said Dad, 'you're a very naughty monkey. *Now give me the key!*'

'Careful, Dad,' I advised. 'Don't panic him.'

'Why not?' said Dad. 'He's panicked me.'

'Let me try.'

I got down on my knees, which is not that easy for me, and looked my little monkey pal in the eyes.

'I know you want to play, Thimble,' I said, but the fact is, that is a very important key, and if Dad doesn't get it, he'll be in a lot of trouble.'

'That's not going to persuade him!' said Dad. 'Tell him *he'll* be in a lot of trouble!'

'Don't think it'll work.'

'Mind out of the way!'

Dad's face appeared beside mine. It was very red and the eyes were rather bloodshot. 'Now look here, old boy!' he barked. 'You give me that key or you are minced monkey meat!'

Thimble backed further into the little prison he had made for himself and placed the key on his tongue.

'He's put it in his mouth!'

'I can see what he's done!'

'Be a good boy, Thimble, and…'

'*Spit it out, you demon!*'

Thimble's mouth closed. His Adam's apple rose and fell.

'I think he's swallowed it, Dad.'

Dad's face turned from red to purple.

'*Open your mouth!*' he cried.

Thimble was happy to do this. There was no key to be seen.

Dad clasped his head in his hands. 'What have I done to deserve this?' he asked.

'Thimble,' I said, 'that was a very naughty thing to do.'

Thimble sniggered, then, seeing my stern face, looked a little guilty.

'We'll have to make him sick,' I said.

'How are we going to do that?' asked Dad.

'They use mustard on dogs.'

'We haven't got mustard! We've only got

bananas! If there's any left, that is!'

There was a call from downstairs. 'Have you got the money yet?'

We trooped down to face PC Bagshaw.

'I'm afraid there's a problem,' said Dad. 'We can't pay you till the monkey's sick.'

'I beg your pardon?' said PC Bagshaw.

'It's a long story. Well, not that long actually. Just embarrassing. Now, how are we going to do this?'

'You could stick your fingers down his throat,' I suggested.

'Are you joking?' said Dad. 'He'll bite them off!'

'What about some kind of shock?' I suggested. 'Shock can make you sick.'

Dad turned to PC Bagshaw. 'Could you say something to scare Thimble?'

'Like what?' asked PC Bagshaw.

'You're a police officer,' said Dad. 'You must know how to scare people.'

PC Bagshaw thought for a moment, then fixed Thimble with a cold-blooded stare. 'Thimble, I arrest you in the name of the law! You're going down for a long time, buddy!'

Thimble cocked his head to one side and adopted a puzzled expression.

'He doesn't understand,' I said.

'Well, I don't know!' snapped PC Bagshaw. 'It's not my job to scare monkeys!'

'Come to think of it,' I said, 'that's a cure for hiccups, not a way of making people sick.'

'I really haven't got time for this,' said PC Bagshaw.

'I know!' said Dad. 'We'll make him car sick!'

'That's a great idea,' I replied. 'Or it would be, if we had a car.'

'We could hire a taxi.'

'That costs money.'

'We'll have money, once he's sick.'

'That's true. Ring Jazzy Cabs, all their drivers drive like nutters.'

'Where to, my friend?' the cab driver asked.

'Just round the block,' said Dad, 'several times probably.'

Dad, Thimble and I climbed into the taxi

and bade our farewells to PC Bagshaw.

'We'll be back in five minutes,' said Dad.

'You'd better be,' said PC Bagshaw.

The taxi pulled smoothly away and proceeded down the road at a steady pace.

'I thought you said these drivers drove like nutters,' said Dad.

'Maybe it's because he saw PC Bagshaw,' I replied.

'Excuse me,' said Dad, 'but is it possible to drive a bit faster?'

'Speed limit, my friend,' said the driver.

'This is hopeless,' said Dad.

'I know,' I said. 'Let's get Thimble to read. Reading makes you car sick.'

'Thimble cannot read,' replied Dad.

'He pretends to, though.'

'Have you got a book?'

'I've always got a book, Dad.' I fished in

my pocket and brought out *Nuff Respect For The Rainbow Posse* by Joe Trendo.

'Not Joe Trendo!' said Dad.

'I like him. He's down with the kids.'

'He's what with the what?'

'He's street smart.'

'Street smart? Everyone knows his real name is Gideon Court-Hampton and he went to the poshest school in the country!'

'You just don't like him because he sells more books than you.'

'Hah! I could sell more books than him, if…'

'If what, Dad?'

'Never mind.'

Silence.

'Are you going to make this monkey sick or aren't you?' said Dad.

With a sigh I opened the book. 'Here you

go, Thims,' I said. 'You look at the pages and I'll read it out for you.'

I held the book in front of Thimble, who seemed to know what was expected of him, and scanned the pages from left to right just as he'd seen me do.

'Is it working yet?' asked Dad.

'Give it time, Dad. It sometimes takes me an hour before reading makes me car sick.'

Dad gave an anxious glance at the taxi meter, which had already notched up a fiver. 'Are you sure you can't go any faster?' he asked the driver.

'Not unless I go on the motorway,' came the reply.

'Then go on the motorway,' said Dad.

'I thought you wanted to go round the block.'

'I've changed my mind. I want to go to

Land's End.'

'Is this wise, Dad?' I said.

'I'll make that monkey sick if it kills me,' said Dad.

County sign followed county sign, the fee on the meter ticked up and up, and still Thimble showed no sign of being sick.

'Are you *sure* he's reading?' said Dad.

'Course he is,' I said. 'Just watch his eyes.'

'Maybe there's something wrong with the book,' said Dad.

'Oh, there's nothing wrong with the book, I replied. We're just getting to the best bit, where the Ghastly Grog gets on a quad bike and the posse...'

'JAMS, I DO NOT WANT TO KNOW!'

'Steady on, Dad. Are you feeling stressed?'

'I AM ABSOLUTELY FINE, THANK YOU!'

'If you say so.'

Dad rapped on the driver's headrest. 'Do you have to drive so smoothly?' he snapped.

'You don't like the way I drive?' came the reply.

'Not really,' said Dad. 'You need to liven things up a bit.'

'And how would you like me to do that?'

'How about going over some hump-backed bridges, really fast, so the car takes off?'

'There are no hump-backed bridges on the motorway, sir.'

'Then get off the motorway and look for some.'

'I thought you wanted to go to Land's End.'

'I've changed my mind. I want to go to the nearest hump-backed bridge.'

The driver viewed Dad in his rear-view mirror. He was no longer looking friendly.

At the next junction he pulled off the motorway, but rather than seek out the nearest hump-backed bridge, he pulled to a halt and turned to face us.

'Are you taking me for a ride?' he asked.

'I thought you were taking us for one,' said Dad.

'Not any more.'

'But we're a hundred miles from home!'

'You pay me, I take you back.'

'We can't pay you till the monkey's sick!'

'I'm sorry?'

'It's very simple. The monkey's got the key to my partner's money box in its stomach and, since you have driven so ridiculously smoothly, he still hasn't sicked it up!'

'What? You're trying to make that monkey sick in my cab?'

'Is that such a big deal?'

'You pay me now or I ring the police!'

Dad raised a hand. 'Just hold your horses, old boy,' he said. 'I need to discuss something with my son.' He leant towards me with a look of grim determination on his face and whispered into my ear. 'Ease your seat belt out very quietly,' he said. 'Then, when I say, open the door and run like hell.'

'What, and leave Thimble?' I said.

'Thimble can cause a diversion.'

I didn't bother to argue, as Dad was well beyond reason, but at the shout of *Now!* I flung open the door and pulled Thimble out with me. Thimble seemed to know what was expected and bolted off into the nearest field like ten devils were after him. I did my best to follow (I actually run better than I walk), and Dad acted as rear gunner, yelling nonsense at the driver such as *Stay Where You Are, There's A Car Thief In The Area!*

Unfortunately, the driver did not seem too worried about car thieves. He was, on the other hand, hell bent on getting his fare from us, though luckily, he had a slight limp and a beer belly even larger than Dad's. Dad himself was going surprisingly well, but obviously this couldn't last. Sure enough, something bad was coming. A dirty great hidden rock. Dad's foot met it full force.

'Hell's bells! I've twisted my ankle!'

'Keep going, Dad!'

'It's agony!'

'But he's catching us!'

Give Dad credit. He really did try to keep going, though one leg was useless and his

face was creased with pain. Eventually, however, he came to a complete halt, folded like a hinge, and went…

BLEURRRCH!

'Oh Dad,' I said, 'you've been sick.'

'Do you think I don't know that?'

'It's funny, us wanting Thimble to be sick, and…'

'NO, IT IS NOT FUNNY!'

'You're right, Dad. Better keep running.'

Dad took a deep breath, tested his ankle, winced, then hobbled on. We'd made another twenty metres or so when, much to my relief, I noticed that the cab driver was no longer chasing. In fact, he had totally disappeared from view.

'Relax, Dad,' I said. 'We've lost him.'

Dad heaved for breath. Thimble ambled back to join us. He was really enjoying this unexpected playtime.

'This is weird,' said Dad. 'That driver was there a second ago.'

'Some kind of Bermuda Triangle?' I suggested. 'Or alien kidnap?'

We scanned the spot where the driver was last seen. It was only now that I noticed that he was actually still there, except flat on the ground. After a while he began to stagger to his feet, looking strangely messy.

Rising to his full height, he shook his hands as if trying to get rid of them, before wiping them on his trousers. Much to our joy, he then stomped back to his cab and drove away.

'Do you know what, Dad?' I said. 'I think he slipped up in your sick.'

'Ha!' said Dad. 'That will teach him to mess with Douglas Dawson!'

I had an idea. 'Do you think,' I said, 'if we show Thimble your sick, it might make him sick?'

'Worth a shot,' said Dad.

We led Thimble back to the fateful spot.

'Look at that, Thims,' I said. 'Isn't it GROSS? All bits of carrot and tomato and ... what is that exactly? Ee-yuck! And as for the smell...'

BLEURRRRCH!

'Hell's bells!' cried Dad. 'All over my
shoes!'

'Sorry, Dad,' I replied.

'Now everyone's been sick but Thimble,'
said Dad.

CHAPTER FOUR
THE DEVIL DRIVES AND
THE MONKEY PUSHES

Getting home was actually quite fun. I'd
never hitched a lift before, but I did what
Dad said and hoicked up my trousers so
people could see my splints. People are
generally very nice to me when they see I'm
disabled and, sure enough, it wasn't long
before a car stopped and offered me a ride.
Mind you, they weren't too happy when
Dad and Thimble jumped out from behind
a bush and climbed in as well.

Not surprisingly, PC Wendy Bagshaw had
not bothered to wait for us. There was just a
sinister-looking letter informing us we had
twenty-four hours to pay our fine. And,

just in case we'd forgotten, there was also a message on the phone reminding us we owed Jazzy Cabs £150.

'Is there any way we can get in touch with Mum?' I asked.

'We do not need your mother!' stormed Dad.

'We need money, that's for sure.'

'There must be some way to make Thimble sick.'

'It's probably too late for that. The key's probably out of his stomach by now and into his duodenum,' I said.

'Do monkeys have duodenums?'

'Of course they do. Except the plural is duodena.'

'You read too much.'

'I have to read, Dad. It's the only way I learn.' I am home-schooled by Dad, except he keeps forgetting to teach me anything.

'Well,' said Dad. 'If we can't make him sick, there's only one way we're going to get the key back now.'

'I don't even want to think about that,' I replied.

'You're going to have to think about it,' said Dad, 'because you're going to do it.'

'What?' I said. 'You're the grown-up!'

'You're his best friend.'

'But I'm allergic to poo,' I protested.

'Just imagine you're looking for a sixpence in a Christmas pudding,' said Dad.

'What? I said. No one puts sixpences in Christmas puddings these days, Dad! What age are you living in?'

'The age when children do as they're told,' said Dad.

I was in the castle kitchen next morning when the door crashed open and there stood Dad, leaning heavily against the doorframe.

'Has he been yet?' he asked.

'Not yet, Dad,' I replied. 'I think he's constipated. Too many bananas. Speaking of which, would you like one for breakfast?'

'I couldn't eat another banana if you paid me,' said Dad.

'No chance of that,' I replied.

Dad gave a loud and painful grunt.

'Are you alright, Dad?' I asked.

'No.'

'God, you look terrible! Your face is like a roadmap.'

'Haven't slept a wink.'

'Why's that?'

'Just look at my foot!'

Dad's sprained ankle was swollen like a grapefruit.

'Wow, Dad. That looks *grievous*!'

'I'll be fine,' said Dad. 'Don't worry about me.'

Dad repeated these phrases several times as he dragged his swollen foot around Dawson Castle, finally reappearing at the kitchen door looking twice as bad as before.

'Are you *sure* there's nothing else to eat?' he asked.

'Nothing,' I replied. 'Well ... except...'

'*What*?'

'No. We couldn't touch that.'

'What?'

I reached into the cupboard, fished about behind the best teapot, and drew out the most precious substance in Dawson Castle:

Mum's Sunday chocolate.

'Maybe you could just have half a piece, like Mum does,' I said, laying the bar on the counter.

Dad studied the little treasure with great interest.

Cavendish and Grieves
Ultimate Luxury Chocolate
85% cocoa solids
with white truffle oil
and candied orchid slivers

'So Mum's kept a little secret from me, has she?' said Dad.

'Please don't tell her I told you, Dad. It's for her special moments after you've gone to bed. She takes a tiny little piece ... (here I began to demonstrate) ... lays it on her

tongue, shuts her eyes, and slowly savours
it like it's the essence of...'

SLOBALOBALOB

My imaginings were interrupted by a
horrible noise like mud sucked down a
drain. When I opened my eyes there was
no sign of the chocolate whatsoever, just an
ugly brown stain round Dad's mouth and

a screwed-up wrapper in his hand. 'What's next?' he grunted.

'Dad! Mum'll be livid!'

'Needs must when the devil drives.'

'I don't even know what that means, Dad, but Mum will still be livid!'

'And I'm still hungry.'

'Well, we've got nothing now. Except the 60p change from the bananas.'

'We could buy taters with that.'

'*Potatoes*. I told you. You'll confuse Thimble. And, anyway, how are you going to get to the shop?'

Dad pondered.

'Have we still got that wheelchair?'

'Yes, Dad.' This was the wheelchair the hospital gave me after I'd had my op, which we'd somehow forgotten to take back.

'I'll go in that.'

'What? I'll never be able to push you!'

'Thimble can do it.'

'Is that wise, Dad?'

'Needs must when the devil drives.'

'Or the monkey pushes.'

'Exactly.'

'I've got a bad feeling about this.'

'Nonsense. It's time that monkey did something to earn his keep.'

Needless to say, Thimble was well up for this new task. Pushing a wheelchair with Dad in it was even more exciting than pushing a trolley. We just had to hope that the results would not be as disastrous.

'Now remember, Thimble,' I said, 'we are going down the shops on Dogsbridge Road, and *nowhere else.*'

'And we are going there to get taters, and *nothing else,*' added Dad.

'No slang, Dad!' I said, for the umpteenth time.

'What does it matter? I'll be the one doing the buying this time.' He opened his hand to show three 20ps, then shut it tight again.

'Wagons roll!' I cried.

We set off up the road, Dad shouting out orders like *Faster! Slower!* and *Left hand down a bit!* After a while, however, the bumpeting motion of the wheelchair seemed to have a lulling effect on him and the orders became less and less frequent, until they finally ceased altogether. To my amazement, he was fast asleep.

'I think he's catching up after his bad night, Thimble,' I said.

Thimble was puzzled. He probably thought this meant a night of being bad. But, before I could explain, Dad's arm

lolled over the side of the chair, his hand
fell open and the three 20ps scattered all
over the pavement. I did my best to rescue
them, but bending down and picking
things up does not come easily to me and,
by the time I had secured the full sixty
pence, Thimble was fifty metres ahead.

'Watch out, Thimble!' I cried. 'There's a…'

I was going to say *hill*, but at that moment
Thimble disappeared over the brow of the
said hill, which was a very steep hill, not
the kind you'd want to push a wheelchair
down without being extremely careful.

I hurried as fast as I could to the top of
the hill, fearing I might see the mangled
wreckage of the wheelchair at the bottom of
it. But there was no sign of the wheelchair,
or Thimble. He must have gone down like
a bolt of lightning. How he'd held on was

anybody's guess. But where was he now?
I don't like being left alone, and it's fair to
say I was in a flat panic walking down that
hill. But I had to keep it together and be
sensible. They were going to buy potatoes
and that meant they were heading for a
fruit and veg shop. Unfortunately, there
were at least three fruit and veg shops on
Dogsbridge Road and no knowing which

one they would aim for. Especially if Dad was still asleep. My only hope was that they would be waiting for me outside one of them. Especially as I had the sixty pence.

I tried every shop, and no luck. I even asked the shop assistants if they'd seen a miserable-looking man being pushed about by a monkey. They said they hadn't and, let's face it, if they had, they would have remembered.

By now I was in a dreadful state. I walked all the way to the end of the shops, all the way back again, looked down every side street, asked dozens of people, then finally sank down on a bench outside the Inkbomb Tattoo Studio, exhausted.

That was when, quite by chance, I caught sight of them.

Inside the tattoo studio.

Thimble had seen me as well. He stood at the window, looking very excited, and beckoned me in. Dad was behind him, still in the wheelchair, still fast asleep.

I went inside and hugged Thimble. 'What are you doing in here?' I asked.

The sound of my voice stirred Dad from his slumber. He opened his eyes, rubbed them, and looked around in some confusion. 'Where am I?' he asked.

'In a tattoo studio, Dad,' I replied.

'What am I doing here?'

'I don't know.'

'Did we get the taters?'

I shook my head. At the same time, Thimble nodded.

'You got the taters, Thimble?' I said. 'How did you do that?'

Thimble pointed happily at the tattoo

artist, busy at work with his needle.

'Hang on...' I said.

The tattooist, seeing Dad was awake, switched off his needle and approached us. 'Ready to settle up now, guys?' he said.

'Settle up?' said Dad. 'What for?'

'The tattoos!' said the tattooist.

'Tattoos?' said Dad. 'What tattoos?'

'On your chest,' said the tattooist.

'Err ... I think I know what's happened,' I said.

Slowly, fearfully, Dad began to unbutton his shirt. Emblazoned across his chest was a big red heart and the slogan I LOVE BANANAS.

'W ... w ... w...' said Dad. Despite being, as he often told us, the world's greatest author, he had completely lost the power of speech.

'You've got a very clever monkey there,'

said the tattooist. 'Explained exactly what you wanted in sign language. That's a hundred quid, please.'

'This is NOT what I wanted!' cried Dad. 'Take it off this minute!'

'That'll be two hundred,' said the tattooist.

Dad looked aghast.

'Can we pay in bananas?' I asked.

CHAPTER FIVE
GRUNTS AND PANTS AND HEALTH AND SAFETY

We did at least get some potatoes for lunch, which Dad would never again call taters, and the tattooist gave us a week to pay him, so we put his bill alongside the bills from Jazzy Cabs and the police, and told ourselves everything would be fine as soon as Thimble did a poo.

Unfortunately, there was still no sign of that happening.

'Maybe we should give Thimble some syrup of figs,' I suggested.

Dad stopped staring dolefully at his tattoo and thought for a moment. 'I think there's some in the Useful Drawer,' he said.

'In the Useful Drawer? What's it doing in there?'

'It's Nora, your mum. You know how disorganised she is.'

I searched in the Useful Drawer. There was no sign of syrup of figs, but I did find something else which made my heart leap.

'Dad!' I cried. 'You remember that wicker corner storage unit we took back to IKEA?'

'I certainly do,' said Dad.

'Well, here's the credit note they gave us! Ten pounds spending money!'

Dad sat bolt upright, fire in his eyes. 'We could buy pickled gherkins with that!' he cried.

'And Swedish meatballs!' I added.

'Fire up the wheelchair! We're back in business, Jams!'

We realised it was a bit of a risk taking Thimble to IKEA. The last time we'd taken him, he'd thought we'd moved house, and we found him asleep in the bedroom section. We were hoping to avoid the bedroom section this time, but Dad couldn't work out how to get to the gherkins without going round the whole store, so that's what we did.

It wasn't long before Thimble started getting confused. As soon as we reached the sofas he assumed we were home, stopped pushing Dad and sat down.

'No, Thimble,' I said. 'We are in a store, remember? Like I explained to you? If this was our house, we wouldn't have twenty-five sofas, or loads of other people wandering round.'

Thimble wasn't convinced. Maybe, in his

childhood home, there were loads of other monkeys wandering round.

'Hmm,' said Dad. 'Maybe we could just leave him here.'

'You're forgetting something,' I said.

'What's that?'

'You need him to push your wheelchair.'

'Ah yes. Oh, bitter fate.'

We moved on, but Thimble's behaviour was becoming increasingly strange. He started hopping from one foot to the other and making strange whining noises. We ignored it at first, but the further we went, the faster the hopping became, until it had become a full-on war dance, accompanied by grunts and pants which were turning everybody's heads.

'What *is* up with you, Thimble?' cried Dad.

'I think he's frustrated he can't sit on anything,' I replied.

'It's driving me nuts,' said Dad. 'Can you take over pushing the wheelchair?'

'I could try I suppose.'

I explained to Thimble he was being

relieved of his duties, but before I could take his job Dad made me make a solemn promise to keep my eyes on Thimble at all times. Dad had been badly scarred by the tattoo episode.

'I promise,' I said.

That wasn't enough for Dad. He made me look him in the eyes, place my hand on my heart and not just promise but *pledge* that I would keep Thimble from any kind of mischief, especially mischief which involved any harm coming to Dad's own person. It really was a very long pledge, and, by the time I had finished making it, Thimble had disappeared.

It was the ultimate nightmare. Thimble at large in IKEA!

'He'll come back,' I said.

'Think of the damage he'll do!' said Dad.

'We'll find him.'

We set off in pursuit of Thimble, looking behind every wall unit, inside every storage box and under every rug. No sign of him. Then, just as we were approaching the bathroom area, my nose detected something unusual and not very pleasant.

'Can you ... smell something, Dad?' I asked.

Dad sniffed. 'Now you mention it,' he said, 'I can.'

'Yuck.'

'Must be something wrong with the drains.'

Before we could investigate further, however, a loud beeping noise rang out across the store, and assistants in yellow appeared from every direction, hastening people towards the exits.

'What's going on?' asked Dad.

'Can you make your way to the checkouts, please, sir?' said the nearest assistant. 'We're evacuating the store.'

'Has there been a bomb scare?' asked Dad.

'Health and safety,' came the reply.

'Health and safety? What does that mean?'

The assistant, who was a nervous-looking young man, did not offer further explanation, so Dad decided to become as difficult as possible.

'Now listen here, old boy,' he said. 'I am not moving from here until I know exactly why I am being moved and, if you're not willing to tell me, you can explain why to my lawyer!'

It was news to me that we had a lawyer, but the threat obviously worked on the young man, who went to fetch the store manager, a no-nonsense woman who looked more up for a fight.

'You'll have to move I'm afraid, sir,' she said.

'Not until you tell me why,' said Dad.

'Very well, sir,' replied the manager. 'A monkey has used a toilet in the bathroom display.'

N0-0-0-0-0-0-0-0-0-0!

'What?' cried Dad. 'That's MY MONKEY! And if he's done a toilet I NEED TO SEE IT!'

The manager remained calm. 'If you go down to the checkouts,' she replied, 'we will bring the monkey to you.'

'No, no, no!' said Dad. 'That's not good enough. I don't just want the monkey. I

WANT HIS POO!'

Dad's epic speech echoed round the store. There was something magnificent and powerful about it, but still the manager held her nerve. 'Just go down to the checkouts, please, sir,' she said.

'Now, listen here. The monkey is my property and therefore anything that comes out of that monkey is ALSO MY PROPERTY. If he'd had a baby, you wouldn't refuse to hand it to me.'

'He hasn't had a baby, sir. Although ... no, let's not go there.'

I could sense Dad was building up to that thing he says, that thing that embarrasses me more than anything on Earth, and sure enough...

'DON'T YOU KNOW WHO I AM?'

'No, sir. Who are you?'

'I AM DOUGLAS DAWSON, THE WORLD-FAMOUS CHILDREN'S AUTHOR!'

'Means nothing to me, sir.'

'MAYBE YOU SHOULD READ MORE OFTEN!'

'I read five books a week, sir. Do you think because I work in a shop I don't read books?'

'I AM DOUGLAS DAWSON, AND I AM NOT MOVING UNTIL YOU HAND ME THAT POO!'

The manager reached for her walkie-talkie. 'Security,' she said.

Within a minute the whole area was swarming with burly security men and women, who definitely looked up for a fight, or maybe several.

'OK,' said Dad, who suddenly looked a

whole lot meeker. 'How about if I give you a stamped-addressed envelope? Then you could send it to me in the post. Have to make sure I put on the postage for a bulky parcel, though. Doubt if it will go through a letterbox.'

'Move down to the checkouts, please, sir,' said the nearest security guard, and this time we did, to be reunited with Thimble, no longer hopping from foot to foot and looking a whole lot happier than we did.

.

CHAPTER SIX
IN WHICH POOH AND PIGLET GO IN SEARCH OF – SORRY, WRONG BOOK

'Let's look at the positives,' I said.

'There are no positives,' said Dad.

'There is one positive,' I replied. 'I don't have to look for the sixpence in the Christmas pudding.'

'You call that a positive?' said Dad. 'I call that a big, fat negative, because it means we've lost the key!'

'We do have the meatballs,' I said.

'And how long are they going to last?' We looked down at his ankle, where the bag of frozen meatballs were resting.

'How's the swelling?'

'Going down, thankfully.'

'There's a positive.'

'Yes, I'll soon be able to walk to jail, which is where I'm heading.'

There was a long silence, during which I began to feel a bit tearful. 'I really think we should get in touch with Mum,' I said.

Suddenly Dad's calmness evaporated. 'I've told you once!' he snapped. 'We do not need your mother!' With that, he stormed from the room and stamped up to the Red Tower, returning minutes later with a small card which he brandished before my eyes.

HANDYMAN AVAILABLE

NO JOB TOO SMALL

CALL 02525 777888

PS, I'm an author really

'Happy now?' said Dad. 'I shall put it in the Post Office window.'

'Why not just put it on the internet? There's this site called FreeAds, and guess what, it's free.'

'I don't trust the internet.'

'I know, Dad. You also think that websites are campsites for spiders.'

'Jams, there is nothing wrong with the Post Office window.'

'It costs money!'

'Not if you don't tell anyone you're putting it there.'

I looked again at the advert. 'What about

Thimble? Can't he be a handyman, too?'

'That,' said Dad, 'would contravene the Trade Description Act.'

'Would what the what?'

'We can't advertise Thimble as a handyman when he's not a man,' explained Dad.

'He's handy, though.'

'At the very least we'd have to advertise him as a handymonkey,' said Dad. 'Which we are not about to do.'

'Hmm,' I said, slipping quietly away to write my own postcard:

HANDYMONKEY AVAILABLE
NO JOB TOO BIG
CALL 02525 777888
PS, he really is a monkey

As it happened we didn't put up either of

the postcards. When we reached the Post Office window a card was already up:

GARDENER WANTED
SMALL JOBS AND BIG JOBS
CALL 02525 888777
Tools and dirt provided

'I can garden,' said Dad.

'I've never seen you garden,' I replied.

'My great-grandad was a gardener,' said Dad. 'Gardens are in my genes.'

Thimble looked puzzled. He knew you could run, jump and skip in gardens, and couldn't understand how this could happen in Dad's jeans. But there was no time for explanations, as Dad was already marching home, not having one of those things he called new-fangled phones you carry around with you.

Half an hour later we stood outside 22 Furlong Road, ready for action. Dad wore his usual outfit, which looked like gardening clothes anyway, and Thimble wore a pair of baggy cords, DIY gloves and grandad's old flat cap.

'I rang about the gardening job,' said Dad, as the door opened.

'Ah yes,' said a woman in a cardigan of many colours. 'Pleased to meet you. I'm Angie Aztec.'

'Douglas Dawson,' said Dad.

The woman's jaw dropped. 'Not *the* Douglas Dawson?'

Dad's jaw dropped, too. 'You've ... heard of me?'

'Of course I've heard of you! I used to be a school librarian.'

'And you've ... read one of my books?'

'All of them.'

Dad's face became so joyful it was almost painful.

'Thank you!' he cried. 'Oh, thank you, thank you, thank you!'

'Let go of her hand, Dad,' I whispered. 'It's embarrassing.'

Dad relaxed his hand just enough for Angie to release her own. 'But ... why are you working as a gardener?' she asked.

'Research,' said Dad.

'Of course,' replied Angie. 'Wait till the girls in the book club hear about this!'

'Book club?'

'Yes, we meet once a fortnight to discuss books. Except I'm going to ring them today to tell them that *the* Douglas Dawson is in my house! With his children!'

'Child, not children. The monkey's no relation.'

Angie put a hand to her mouth. 'Oh, my goodness!' she cried. 'I am sorry! I hadn't even realised it was a monkey!'

'I had to bring him,' explained Dad. 'He can't be left on his own.'

'Oh, don't apologise! How wonderfully

eccentric and author-like, to keep a monkey!'

'Err ... thank you.'

'Would you do us a huge favour and sign some books for us? The girls will be thrilled!'

'If I'm not too busy,' said Dad.

'Oh, you won't be too busy,' said Angie. 'I shall give you one little job, then it will be meet-the-author time!'

The job, it turned out, was very simple. Dad was to dig a hole, a very deep hole, place a young cherry tree in it, then fill the hole with a mix of earth and manure. The manure was ready and waiting in a wheelbarrow, and POO, it sure did stink! I do not like bad smells and this was capital-B Bad. Thimble, however, seemed quite fascinated by the wheelbarrow and its contents. Maybe it reminded him of a supermarket trolley. The barrow, that is, not the contents.

If Dad could smell the horrible stink he showed no sign of it. As soon as Angie had left to phone her friends he seized a shovel and began digging.

'Look at this, Jams!' he cried. 'A true man of the soil! I think I may take my shirt off!'

Dad began unbuttoning his shirt, then remembered the colourful artwork adorning his chest.

'Maybe not,' he said.

'What am I supposed to do?' I asked.

'Find a little fork and do some weeding.'

'What about Thimble?'

'Just keep him out of trouble.'

I did as requested, taking Thimble a good

distance from Dad's hole. 'Come on Thims,' I said. 'We'll pull up the dandelions.'

Thimble tensed.

'Dandelions are not actually a kind of lion,' I explained.

Thimble relaxed.

'They do sound like lions that dress up,' I admitted.

Thimble tensed again.

'But they're actually weeds.'

Thimble relaxed again.

I can't squat, but I can kneel, and pretty soon I was weeding like a pro. Thimble started quite well, but was soon getting distracted by the wheelbarrow. Every few seconds he looked round at it, and while he was looking round he was pulling up daffodils instead of dandelions.

'Alright, Thimble,' I said. 'I'll take you to

the wheelbarrow. You can have a good look at it, then you can concentrate on what you're supposed to be doing. OK?'

Thimble happily followed me to the very smelly barrow.

'There, Thimble. That is a wheelbarrow. And inside the wheelbarrow is manure. You don't need to know what manure is, Thimble. Well, OK, it's something which comes out of a horse's bottom and helps plants to grow. Now, you see the big hole that Dad is digging? That's where the manure is going. Satisfied now?'

Thimble nodded eagerly.

'Good. Now let's get back to weeding. And no looking round!'

We got back to work. By now Dad was halfway to Australia and you couldn't even see the top of his head, but I knew he was happy because he was singing. Dad doesn't often sing, and when he does it's always *I Was Born Under A Wandering Star*, a song written in about 1850 when he was born. Thimble, however, was still not content. After a few minutes' weeding he glanced round at the wheelbarrow again, then again, then again and again and again. This was starting to drive me mad.

'Do you want to push the wheelbarrow, Thimble?' I asked.

Thimble nodded eagerly.

'OK,' I said. 'You can push the wheelbarrow *once* round the garden. Just *once*, is that clear? Then I want you to come back here and completely forget about it.'

Thimble did not need a second invitation. He lolloped eagerly to the barrow and, with some difficulty, lifted the arms. With such a heavy load, pushing wasn't easy, but Thimble is a canny monkey and soon got it balanced. With some relief, I returned to my weeding.

'Just once, remember,' I said, but I need not have worried. Thimble was as good as his word and in a minute was back beside me.

'Good boy, Thimble,' I said. 'Err ... where's the barrow?'

Thimble pointed enthusiastically at the area where Dad was digging his hole. Ah yes. There was the wheelbarrow. Except ... something was missing.

'Thimble,' I said. '*Where is the manure?*'

At this point I noticed that Dad was no longer singing.

'*Thimble, you haven't…*'

My words were interrupted by the sudden

and noisy arrival in the garden of Angie Aztec's Book Club.

'I've never met a real-life author!' said the first woman.

'I'm sure he's just as normal as you and me,' said the second.

'Where is he, exactly?' said the third.

'Jams,' said Angie, 'do you know where your dad is?'

'Err,' I said, pointing vaguely at the spot where Dad had been digging. 'I think he's over there.'

All eyes turned to the said spot. Right on cue, a horrible hand, caked in gunk, shot up above the edge of the hole and groped frenziedly for a hold. As it seized hard on a clump of grass a second scrabbling hand appeared, followed by a gruesome, rotten face with staring bloodshot eyes.

'That BEEP monkey! When I get hold of it, I'll BEEP its BEEP BEEP till it's BEEP BEEP BEEP!'

'Oh my word,' said the first woman.

'What on Earth?' said the second.

'I've just remembered, I've got shopping to do,' said the third.

With superhuman effort, the zombie

mud-man hauled himself out of the hole, rose to his full height and began staggering towards the women, filthy hand outstretched.

'Sorry about the language,' he croaked. 'Who wants an autograph?'

The women began backing away.

'I've got my special signing pen,' said the zombie.

The women fled, pursued by Dad as far as the French windows, which were abruptly shut in his face.

'It's a Parker!' wailed Dad. 'A top-of-the-range Parker pen!'

Sadly, in the space of half an hour, Dad had both found and lost the only fan club he'd ever had.

CHAPTER SEVEN
WEE WILLIE WINKIE AND THE DINOSAUR'S REVENGE

The Great Hall in Dawson Castle had become just like a High Court. Thimble sat on a rude stool like a common criminal, facing Dad, who occupied his favourite and most important armchair, wearing the weighty frown of a Lord Chief Justice.

'I have tried with you, Thimble,' he said. 'Believe me, I have tried. I have given you shelter and clothing and food, and what have you done in return? You have thrown it back in my face.'

'He's never thrown food in your face!' I protested.

'He threw something in my face, that's for sure!'

'He didn't do it on purpose. He acts on instinct.'

'What nonsense! A monkey has an instinct to eat bananas and run from snakes! A monkey does not have an instinct to bury a man in horse's dung!'

Dad's angry voice was unsettling Thimble. He hopped off his chair, scuttered round behind Dad, and began picking at his hair. 'Stop that!' cried Dad. 'What are you doing?'

'He's looking for nits,' I replied.

'I do not have nits! And if I did I would not want him picking them!'

'It's Thimble's way of showing respect, Dad.'

'He should have shown respect back in the garden!'

'He won't do it again.'

'You're darned right he won't, because I'm never going near a garden again.'

'Oh, Dad! Don't give up! You were brilliant at gardening!'

Dad punched his knee with alarming force. 'No one wants my *gardener's* autograph!' he moaned.

'No, but gardeners do get paid,' I replied.

'Writers get paid! And I'm a writer! Look, I've got a signing pen!'

'Yes, Dad.'

'And I am going to use it,' he declared. 'I'm going to use so much, I'll need to buy a refill!'

'What are you on about, Dad?'

Dad's eyes narrowed. 'Jams,' he said, 'do you remember I said that someone wants to publish my books?'

'Yes, Dad. But they wanted something from you that you didn't want to give.'

'Till now.'

'You've changed your mind?'

'Yes.'

'Dad, who are these people?'

Dad's eyes darted from side to side, as if to check no one was listening. 'The Spoogies,' he said.

'The whatties?'

'The Spoogarian Foundation, to give them their full name.'

'They sound like a religious cult.'

'I prefer to call them a faith group.'

'They sound weird.'

'They are weird.'

'So what is it they want from you?'

'Oh, nothing.'

'It can't have been nothing, Dad, or it wouldn't have bothered you so much.'

'Forget about it, Jams. I was just being fussy. Now, keep that monkey occupied while I go up to the Red Tower and sort them out a bestseller!'

An hour passed and I began to wonder if Dad had fallen asleep, as often happened when he went up to write. But no, I found him at the computer, concentrating hard.

'*This* is the one I shall be submitting,' said Dad. '*My Gerbil Died Last Night*.'

'Sounds a bit heavy,' Dad.

'It's important that children learn about the realities of life. And death.'

'What's the story, Dad?'

'Well, there's this little boy, Rams, who gets a gerbil for his birthday. But the gerbil is obsessed with this monster, called the Tuffalo, and goes out to the woods to fight it. To cut a long story short, the rodent gets eaten.'

'Wow, Dad. That is heavy.'

'Yes, but this is where it gets interesting, Jams. I wanted to make it educational, so the rest of the story is basically the gerbil's journey through the Tuffalo's digestive system.'

'And ... is there a happy ending?'

'No, Jams, because there are not always happy endings in life. However, when it reaches the lower bowel, hey presto, a pop-up page. No one will be expecting that!'

Dad's face was filled with happiness, but at the same time there was a weird, pleading look in his eyes, as if he was desperate for me to reassure him.

'Sounds ... great, Dad,' I said.

'I'm glad you think so!' said Dad. 'I'm glad you think so because I know the Spoogies will think so, too! Now, they say I must not send it by snail mail, but by eel mail. Any idea what that means?'

'E-mail maybe?' I suggested.

'I'm fairly sure it was eel mail.'

'I'm fairly sure it wasn't.'

'I'll tell you what, Jams. I'll give you the address and you send it.'

Dad duly gave me the address, and I duly sent his masterpiece.

'Good luck, Dad,' I said, looking forward to getting back downstairs to Thimble, who suddenly seemed the very model of sanity.

Mum calls me the world's greatest optimist, but I wasn't very optimistic about Dad's chances. So imagine my surprise when Dad burst into the room, less than two hours later, and planted a big kiss on my forehead.

'Put out the flags, Jams,' he cried. 'We're in business!'

'They took the story?'

'They sure did!'

'Wow! That was quick!'

'They loved it, Jams! Had to make a few edits, mind.'

'I hope the pop-up page survived.'

'No, that's gone.'

'The fight with the Tuffalo?'

'Err…'

'You've cut the fight with the Tuffalo?'

'Yes, Jams, but I have added things.'

'What kind of things?'

'Never you mind. Listen, they've sent me a contract, and I must run it off and sign it before they arrive.'

'They're coming here? Tonight?'

'Relax, Jams. We'll be finished before midnight.'

'What? This sounds like Cinderella!'

'That's right, Jams. A fairy tale come true. Now, how do I print off this contract?'

'On the printer, Dad.'

'Printer?'

'That big black box by the computer.'

'Ah. That's what that's for.'

'Don't worry, Dad. I'll do it.'

'OK. But no reading the contract, or the story.'

Things were starting to smell awfully fishy, but I went along with Dad's wishes, and Thimble helped by feeding the paper into the printer, while Dad stood alongside beaming happily and saying things like 'So *that's* how it's done!' and 'Do you know, Thimble, I'm starting to see the funny side of being covered in dung!'

'There you go. All done.'

'Excellent,' said Dad. 'Now all I need to do is to sign it. Do you have a pin, Jams?'

'A pin? Do you mean a pen?'

'No, Jams. I mean a pin.'

'Err ... there's one in Grandma's old sewing box.'

'Of course.'

Dad disappeared with the contract. Hmm, I thought. Maybe I could just slightly break my promise and read a little bit of *My Gerbil Died Last Night*.

I gave the mouse a little shake and brought up Dad's story. Hmm, I thought again. The last page would be a good place to start:

A single tear dropped onto the little shoebox in which lay my beloved Nigella. Never again would she burrow into her pile of wood shavings or gnaw on her favourite toilet roll. But though Nigella's little heart had stopped, her soul lived on in Bob Special's cosmic playground where soon we would once more be united.

Yikes, I thought. What was *that* about? Maybe I should take a peek at the rest of the story...

Too late. Dad was returning with the contract. 'All done,' he said.

I studied Dad's signature. 'Why did you sign in red felt tip?' I asked.

Dad did not reply. I looked closer.

'Hang on ... is this *blood*?'

'Can't remember,' said Dad.

'You *can't remember* if you signed the contract in blood?'

'I may have done.'

My eyes fell on the final sentences of the contract, just above the signature:

i. I hereby grant the Spoogarian Foundation worldwide rights over all my future writing.

ii. I pledge my immortal soul to our eternal saviour Bob Special.

'Dad!' I cried. 'What on earth are you doing? You don't even believe in souls!'

'Exactly, so where's the problem?'

'This is crazy!'

'Listen, son. They are paying me one thousand pounds up front. One thousand pounds, Jams! I'll be able to pay off the police fine, the taxi fare, the tattooist, and still have change for some taters – er, potatoes!'

There was a grumble of thunder in the night sky, followed by a crack of lightning, which lit up the side of Dad's face like some awful Halloween mask.

'I don't like this, Dad,' I said.

'You don't have to,' said Dad.

'What would Mum say?'

'Mum isn't here. Now, go and put on your best suit and find a DVD for Thimble. I don't want to see or hear a sound from him until everything is signed and sealed.'

CHAPTER EIGHT
THE END OF THE WORLD AND A GOOD BOOK SALE

I did my best with Thimble. I put him in his banana pyjamas, found *Big Trucks and Monster Machines* (his favourite DVD) and promised him a special treat if he sat still and quiet until further notice. Thimble, as we know, is not especially good at staying still and quiet, but he hadn't forgotten being put on trial and was doing his best to behave. I was quite sure he would do nothing to mess up Dad's important meeting.

Then again, I am the world's greatest optimist.

Dad was doing all he could to prepare

Dawson Castle for his guests. He'd put out two of our best chairs and a side table, on which were placed two glasses of water and two halves of a banana. Frankly it looked a bit sad, but I didn't say that, because Dad was so full of hope and expectation.

Meanwhile the night grew stormier, and the loose parts of Dawson Castle rattled like giant dice in a tin bath. I felt a deep sense of foreboding, which is a long word for apprehensiveness. When a great knock finally came on the West Door, it took all my willpower not to flee to my room. But I stayed strong and put on a brave smile as Dad welcomed the Spoogies into our abode.

There were three of them, dressed in the whitest white shirts, the blackest black suits and the shiniest shiny shoes. Their

heads were so clean they could have been
boiled for a week, and each carried a sleek,
silver briefcase. But that was where the
similarities ended, because the man in
front was as tall and thin as a beanpole, and
the men behind were as short and squat as
beanbags.

'I'm so sorry,' said Dad. 'I've only put out two chairs. I don't know why, I thought there'd be two of you. Maybe someone could sit on someone's lap?'

Dad obviously meant this as a joke, but no one laughed.

'That is strictly against our beliefs,' said the tall man. 'Even for married couples.' He had an accent which was part British, part American, part telephone answering machine.

'Maybe you could give up your seat, Jams?' said Dad.

I began to rise. The tall man's eye fell on my splints. I'm used to people looking at my splints and wondering what they are for. If they ask me I tell them they're to keep my feet flat. *Aha*, they say, and go on their way. But this man's look was different. It was as if my splints were a pair of poisonous snakes.

'No, that's all right, thank you,' he said.

'This is my son, Jams, by the way,' said Dad.

'Good evening, young man,' said the man. 'You may call me Topher Spoog the Elder.' He didn't look into my eyes but slightly to the side of my head, as if I had another head there.

'Howdy,' I replied, but the Spoogies were already discussing who would sit where, finally deciding that Topher Spoog the Elder would take the first seat and the short ones would stand either side of him.

'Water?' said Dad.

'No, thank you,' came the reply.

'Banana?'

'We'd like to get on with the business,

please, Mr Dawson.'

'Of course.' Dad handed Topher Spoog the contract, which he scanned eagerly, a secret smile emerging as he arrived at Dad's signature.

'Excellent,' said Topher Spoog. 'And here is your advance, Mr Dawson.' He opened his briefcase, which to my amazement, was packed full of banknotes. He loaded these, one wad after another, on to the side table while Dad hurriedly moved the water and bananas to make room for them.

'Wow,' said Dad. 'Can I touch them?'

'They are yours, Mr Dawson.'

Dad picked up one of the wads and gave it a deep and worshipful sniff.

'There,' said Topher Spoog. 'That will pay off your police fine.'

'How do you know about our police fine?'

asked Dad.

'We have friends everywhere,' replied Topher Spoog.

Outside a flash of lightning was immediately followed by a roll of thunder, indicating that we were now at the very centre of the storm.

'I can't wait to see this book,' said Dad.

'Wait no more,' replied Topher Spoog. He nodded to the man on the left, who opened his own briefcase, took out a shiny new book, and handed it to Dad.

The book was *My Gerbil Died Last Night*.

'Wow,' said Dad. 'You guys move fast.'

'We have to move fast,' replied Topher Spoog. 'Tonight is Odd Fellows Eve, the beginning of the Endtime.'

'Endtime?'

'Yes, the end of the earth. Two weeks tonight.'

'Wow,' I said. 'That sounds depressing.'

'Oh no! It's not depressing at all!' replied Topher Spoog. 'Once the Invisigoths have sacked the Earth, the followers of Bob Special will swim in the ocean of goodness with the angels of permanence!'

There was a huge smile on his mouth, but an equally huge frown on his forehead, as if his face was having a fight with itself.

'What about everyone else?'

'They will be trapped in the cosmic elevator with the foul breath of the Twisted Sisters.'

'That doesn't sound good.'

'That is why we must convert them now. With the help of this book.'

Dad gazed in wonderment at the slim volume in his hands. 'But won't it take a while to get it into the bookshops?' he asked.

'Bookshops?' replied Topher Spoog. 'We

don't need bookshops! We have an army of followers ready and willing to take this book to every doorstep in the land!'

'Wow,' said Dad. 'That should be good for sales.'

'We are printing seventy thousand and seventy-seven.'

'Seventy thousand and seventy-seven? But ... that will put me on top of the bestseller charts!'

It will indeed.

'Only for one week though, Dad,' I said. 'Because then the world will end.'

Dad wasn't listening. His eyes were glued to *My Gerbil Died Last Night* and the Spoogies clearly had him in the palms of their hands. 'I'd like to meet this Bob Special,' he said, 'and thank him personally.'

'Bob Special is with the angels,' replied

Topher Spoog.

'Oh,' said Dad. 'I'm sorry. I didn't realise.'

'Bob Special was betrayed. He drank twenty pints of beer which the devil had convinced him was water.'

'That's unfortunate.'

'But, never fear, you shall still meet him. Tonight.'

'Tonight? Err ... how's that?'

'Because tonight is Odd Fellow's Eve, when he has promised to return. We do not know in what form he will return, but return he shall, to lead us all in the Endtime.'

'Excellent,' said Dad. 'That should be good for sales, too.'

Topher Spoog took a deep, deep breath. 'I am feeling him in this room,' he said. 'I am feeling him now.'

'Come, Bob!' said the other Spoogies.

'Chant with us,' said Topher Spoog.

He held both hands out, as if grasping an invisible, giant fruit bowl. The other Spoogies did the same. Dad laid down *My Gerbil Died Last Night* and, with just a little embarrassment, took hold of his own invisible bowl.

'Come, great leader, and show thyself!' chanted Topher Spoog.

'Come, great leader, and show thyself!' chanted the other Spoogies.

'Come, err, you know, and err, what they said,' chanted Dad.

'*Come, great leader, and show thyself!*' chanted all three Spoogies together, louder and louder and louder, till Dad's voice rose EVEN LOUDER, and yea, every picture began to shake, every ornament began to rattle, the heavens erupted with thunder, the door crashed open, and in walked Thimble.

There was a great gasp from the Spoogies.

'Is it thou, Bob?' asked Topher Spoog. 'Show us a sign!'

Thimble pointed to his head and made two circles with his finger.

'Thank the heavens!' cried Topher Spoog, dropping to his knees. 'He has returned!'

The other Spoogies also dropped to their knees and thanked the heavens. It all seemed the greatest game in the world to Thimble, who began bouncing up and down, waving his arms and gibbering.

'He speaks in tongues!' cried Topher Spoog. 'What are you saying to us, great leader?'

Thimble made the sign for *I need the toilet*.

'Of course, great one!' said Topher Spoog.

'We will take you to your people!'

I'd had enough of this. 'Now listen here,'
I said. 'This is not Bob Special. This is
Thimble, and he's part of *our* family, and *my*
best friend, and he's not going anywhere!'

Topher Spoog became very serious. He
rose to his full height, and as he did so his
eyes fell again on my splints. What *was* his
problem? Was wearing splints against his
religion?

'This is beyond your understanding, young man,' he said.

'He's not going anywhere,' I repeated.

Topher Spoog turned to Dad. 'The great one must come with us,' he said.

'Um...' said Dad. 'I'm not questioning your beliefs, but on this one occasion I think you may have made a...'

'How much money do you want?' asked Topher Spoog.

'It's not a matter of money...'

'We will give you seventy thousand and seventy-seven pounds,' said Topher Spoog.

'For Thimble? *Seventy* thousand?'

'And seventy-seven.'

'Blimey. That's a lot of money.'

'Don't listen to them, Dad!' I cried. But to my dismay I could see that greed and ambition were working like poison in his veins.

'Can I ... see this money?' he asked.

'We will bring it at the first crack of dawn,' replied Topher Spoog. 'And, in return, you must hand us the great one.'

'OK,' said Dad.

'NO-O-O-O-O-O-O-O!' I cried.

'Until the dawn,' said Topher Spoog.'

CHAPTER NINE
THE GHOST OF A FLEA AND THE CHEST OF A SHIP

'You can't, Dad!' I cried. 'You just *can't*!'

'Relax, Jams,' said Dad. 'The world won't end in two weeks. They'll realise Thimble isn't this Bob Special person, and they'll sell him back to us for half the price. In the meantime, we'll have paid off all our debts and I will be number one in the bestseller charts!'

'But Dad, how do you know they'll sell him back? They might decide he's the devil in disguise, and then what will they do to him?'

'Oh, come on, Jams, what happened to the great optimist? Everything will be just fine.'

'You don't *know* that!'

'Everything will be just fine,' repeated Dad, patting his copy of *My Gerbil Died Last Night*.

'I hate that book,' I said.

'You'll learn to love it,' said Dad.

'Why should I?' I cried. 'You never learned to love Thimble!'

Back in my room, Thimble was fast asleep in the laundry basket. Thimble had always slept in my room, apart from his first night in Dawson Castle, when he slept in Dad's bed and Dad slept in the dog kennel. To live without him would be unthinkable, hopeless, utter emptiness; like living alone on the moon.

I switched on my phone and rang Mum's number.

I'm sorry I'm not here to take your call right now, said that oh-so-familiar voice. *Please leave your message after the tone.*

'Mum?' I said. 'I know you said not to call unless there was an emergency, but this is an emergency! Dad has sold Thimble! They're coming for him at dawn! If you get this message, please come home as quick as you can! Love you, Mum.'

Ringing Mum tipped me over the edge. I started to cry like a baby. Crying can make you feel better, but sometimes it just makes you feel sick and exhausted, because the reason for crying hasn't gone away and there is nothing you can do but carry on suffering. So I lay on my bed and hoped for sleep, although there was little chance of that.

Mum says I am a creative genius because

I can think up such great stories, but
sometimes imagination can stop being your
friend and turn into your worst enemy.
This was such a time. I imagined Thimble
lost and confused, unable to understand
what his best friends had done to him. I
imagined Topher Spoog, furious that the
world hadn't ended, looking for someone

to blame. I imagined the Spoogies seizing Thimble and…

I threw back the duvet and sat up in bed. I didn't know what I would do, or what I would say, but I took a torch and went back up to the Red Tower.

'Dad?'

There was a grunt.

'Are you awake?'

'Evidently.'

'Why's that?'

'Too much sugar in my cocoa.'

'Can I have a book to read?'

'You've got a room full of books!'

'I've read them all. Several times, some of them.'

'I don't have children's books up here.'

'I'll read anything.'

'Except *My Gerbil Died Last Night*.'

'Yes, except that.'

'Goodnight then.'

I stayed.

'Aren't there some books in your ship's chest? You told me you kept some books there. From your childhood.'

'Hurry up then,' said Dad. 'Just pick one and let me get some sleep.'

I opened the chest, which wasn't easy as the hinges were ancient and groaned like a sick goat. In the light of my little torch I made out some flaky old paperbacks: *Moldy Warp the Mole*, *Five Children and It*, *Emil and the Detectives*, *The Wheel on the School*.

'*The Wheel on the School*?' I said. 'What's that about?'

'Dunno,' said Dad. 'Never read it.'

'Why did you buy it?'

'My dad gave it to me when he had my cat put down.'

'That's sad.'

'It was a long time ago.'

'Why did he have it put down?'

'I thought you were looking for a book.'

'I am.'

I delved deeper into the ship's chest and my hands came across a battered old folder. OLD WRITING it said, in handwriting a bit like Dad's, except less angry looking.

I opened it and pulled out a wodge of papers, held together by a bulldog clip. On the front of this wodge were the words THE GHOST OF A FLEA BY DOUG K. DAWSON, not printed, but typed.

Wow, I thought. This really is old.

As Dad was not watching, I turned the page, and began to read.

I don't know how much time had passed. When I'm reading I go into a magic universe where there is no such thing as time. I came back to Earth when Dad called my name, and it was only then I realised I'd read eight chapters of *The Ghost of a Flea*. It was nothing like anything I'd ever read. I couldn't believe Dad had written it.

'Jams,' said Dad. 'It's 3am. You have got to go to bed.'

'I'm reading something, Dad. Something by you.'

'I thought you were reading *The Wheel on the School*.'

'No, Dad. I'm reading *The Ghost of a Flea*.'

'What? I never said you could read that!'

'It's nothing like your other stories, Dad.'

'I should hope not. I wrote it when I was eighteen.'

'I really like it.'

'Yes, well, you're young.'

'So?'

'You don't realise how immature it is.'

'I don't think it's immature. It's just ... honest.'

'I should have burnt it.'

'No, Dad! People should read it! It's so full of life, and hope, and ... it's brilliant, Dad.'

Dad sat up in bed. 'Hand it here,' he said. I did so, and held the torch over the pages so Dad could read them. Soon, like me, he was turning one after the other, a frown of concentration on his face. When he finally put down the pile of papers that frown was deeper than ever.

'I don't remember writing a word of this,' he said.

'But you did write it?'

'Yes.'

My eyes fell on the bedside table, on which lay *My Gerbil Died Last Night*. 'And now you're writing this,' I said.

Dad did not reply.

'What happened, Dad?'

'Life happened.'

'That sounds bleak.'

'Everyone gets worn down.'

'I hope I don't.'

'Maybe you won't.'

'Well, don't sell Thimble then, because if I lose Thimble, I'll lose hope!'

Again, Dad did not reply, but behind me I could hear a soft padding on the stairs. I don't know if Thimble had heard his name or just woken and found I wasn't in the room but, sure enough, in he came. He sat himself on Dad's lap, put his arms around his neck, and rested his head against his chest.

'Don't sell Thimble, Dad,' I said.

Wearily, Dad lay back down, and Thimble went with him. There was just enough room for me to sneak alongside them and finally get to sleep.

CHAPTER TEN
WARM KITTENS AND BANANAS MEANS BANANAS

The hammering on the door would have woken the dead. The Spoogies had arrived, just as they had promised, at the crack of dawn.

But where was Dad? And – oh no – where was Thimble?

I clambered out of Dad's bed and hurried downstairs, still in pyjamas, with all the speed I could muster. Dad was already at the West Door.

'No, Dad!' I cried. 'Don't open it!'

Too late. The door was open and Dad was face to face with Topher Spoog. In Spoog's hand was a large metal case and beside him were his two squat companions. Behind these, to my horror, were about a hundred more Spoogies.

'Good morning, Mr Dawson,' said Topher Spoog. 'What a glorious day!'

Dad looked outside. It was dull and grey and a little bit drizzly.

'For those with eyes to see,' added Topher Spoog.

I came up alongside Dad. Topher Spoog gave me a half-second smile then refocused

on Dad. 'This, Mr Dawson,' he said, 'is for you.' So saying, he placed the large metal case on the ground, unlocked it, and revealed a solid mass of fifty pound notes, shining like they'd been printed yesterday.

I had never seen anything half as sinister.

'We have kept our side of the deal,' said Topher Spoog. 'Now you must keep yours.' Dad gazed long and hard at the massive hoard of money, then took a deep breath.

'I've changed my mind,' he said.

'Yes!' I cried.

'*What*?' cried Topher Spoog.

'You heard me,' said Dad.

'Have you forgotten your contract with us?' said Topher Spoog.

'It's not worth the paper it's written on,' said Dad.

'Hand us Bob Special!' cried Topher Spoog, and immediately the whole crowd broke into a mighty chant of *Bob! Bob! Bob!*

'His name is Thimble,' said Dad. 'And he is staying right here, so you can give your stupid money back to the poor deluded fools it came from! Thank you and goodbye!'

With that, Dad slammed the West Door shut. 'Wind down the portcullis, Jams,' he said. 'And prepare to resist all boarders!'

'Wow, Dad,' I said. 'That was awesome! Where's Thimble?'

'Locked him in the dungeon,' said Dad. This wasn't as bad as it sounds. The dungeon was what Dad called the toilet, and Thimble sometimes played in there for hours, pressing on the ballcock to make the cistern fizz. Sure enough, he was playing happily when we found him and I gave him a big, loving hug.

'You won't understand this, Thimble,' I said, 'but Dad just did something totally wicked and now everything's going to be hunky dory!'

'The looks on their faces!' said Dad. 'To think they thought that Douglas K. Dawson could be bought for a few pieces of silver.'

'Yes, to think they thought that! Although, to be fair, Dad, I thought it too for a while.'

'They'll be going home with their tails between their legs!'

'They sure will.' I glanced through the dungeon window. 'Although, actually, Dad ... they're not going.'

Dad came to the window. The Spoogies

spotted him and there was a great clamour and shaking of fists, followed by a clod of earth hitting the window.

'Who did that!?' cried Dad.

Almost immediately a whole shower of clods followed.

'Hell's bells!' cried Dad. 'Dawson Castle is under siege!'

The word *siege* struck terror into me. I knew all about sieges: the trebuchets, the mangonals, the battering rams and, worst of all, the dead animals flung over the castle walls to spread typhoid and plague.

'Quick, Dad! Ring the police!'

Dad did so. 'Hello?' he said. 'This is Douglas Dawson, the famous writer, of Dawson Castle! We're under attack from my publishers! They're trying to steal our monkey!'

'Yes, that's right, the monkey that chopped down the telegraph pole... No, I haven't paid the fine yet, but I've got the money and… Yes, he did also demolish the police station, but that was ages ago... Hello? Hello? *Hello*?'

Dad stared at the phone in disbelief. 'They hung up,' he said.

'Now what are we going to do?' I asked.

'Get Thimble up at the window, 'said Dad. 'We've got to prove he's not this Bob Special come back to life.'

'How are we going to do that?'

'You'll think of something.'

'*I'll* think of something?'

'You're always telling me your ideas are better than mine.'

'But I'm scared, Dad! There's so many of them!'

'Never be scared of a full house, Jams.'

I went to the window, opened it, and called Thimble over. The moment he appeared, a forest of hands shot into the air, accompanied by a mighty roar, followed by cries of *Bob! Bob! Bob!*

'Listen!' I cried, not expecting anyone to actually listen, except they did. 'Err...' I said. 'This isn't Bob Special.'

Howls of outrage, shaking fists, cries of *No!*

'If this was Bob Special,' I said, 'would he do this?'

I turned to Thimble. 'Now, Thimble,' I said, 'I want you to pick your nose, like we always tell you not to, pull out a big slithery bogey, which normally you must never do, and eat it!'

Thimble did as he was told.

The crowd fell completely silent.

'There!' I said. 'Doesn't that…'

No one was listening. No one was listening because they were all picking their own noses, pulling out whatever was inside, and eating it.

Bob! Bob! Bob! came the cry, louder than ever.

'This isn't working,' I said.

'They'll get fed up and go home eventually.'

'I don't think so.'

I moved away from the window, taking Thimble with me, hoping this might calm the Spoogies down. But, no, it only made them more manic. The hubbub grew and grew, until suddenly there was an almighty crash at the front door.

'They've got a battering ram!' I cried.

'It's ... the telegraph pole!' said Dad.

'They must have got it from the police!'

'They said they had friends everywhere!'

CRASH! The whole of Dawson Castle shuddered.

'That door's had it!' cried Dad.

'What are we going to do?'

'Hide Thimble!' said Dad.

At the sound of this, Thimble began leaping about the room and chattering manically.

'He's panicking!' I cried. 'We'll never keep him quiet!'

'Then we've had it!' said Dad.

At this point I realised that, however panicky I was feeling, Dad was ten times worse. If we were going to get out of this situation, it was down to me. With Thimble's future, maybe his life, in my hands, my mind became amazingly decisive. I hatched a plan, possibly a very foolish one, but a plan nevertheless.

'Strap on my splints, Dad,' I said. 'I'm going into battle.'

'Are you sure?' asked Dad.

'Dad,' I replied, 'just do as you're told.'

Dad did as he was told and, breathing as steadily as possible, I made my way to the West Door, just as it received another massive battering. It was only then I realised that I'd put on my splints and shoes while still wearing my pyjamas, but nothing could stop me now. I unlocked the door and stepped outside.

Topher Spoog raised an arm. The crowd fell silent and the men with the battering ram stood still.

'If you're hoping to make a deal with us,

young man,' he said, 'you can forget it.'

'I'm not here to offer you a deal,' I said. 'I'm here to offer you a challenge.'

'You want to challenge *us*?' said Topher Spoog, laughing.

'I want to challenge *you*,' I replied.

Topher Spoog's face hardened. 'Do you not know who I am?' he said. 'I am Topher Spoog, Supreme Elder of the Spoogarian Foundation, anointed and appointed by his ultimate holiness, Bob Special!'

'And I am Jams Cogan,' I replied, 'anointed and appointed by Thimble Monkey Superstar!'

'You are nothing but a feeble child,' said Topher Spoog.

'I'm stronger than you,' I replied.

'There is nothing stronger than the spirit of Bob Special,' said Topher Spoog.

The crowd howled their agreement. I addressed them. 'I will prove to you all that I am stronger than this man!' I cried.

'And how do you propose to do that?' asked Topher Spoog.

'We will stand toe to toe,' I replied, 'and see who takes a backward step first.'

'Ha!' said Topher Spoog. He straightened to his full height, folded his arms and waited, a confident smile playing on his lips. I hobbled forward and took up position opposite him.

Absolute silence.

I reached down and tightened a strap on my splint. Topher Spoog glanced down at it. A flicker of anxiety crossed his face.

'It's not catching, you know,' I said.

'What?' he said.

'My disability.'

Ever-so-slowly, I lifted my arm.

Topher Spoog watched it.

I moved my hand towards him.

His brows knitted.

Very gently, my hand took hold of his.
It was as if I'd given him an electric shock.
His hand shot away and, in that same
instant, he stepped backwards.

'What are you scared of, Topher?' I said.

Too late, Topher Spoog realised what had
happened.

'You cheated!' he cried.

'No, I didn't.'

Topher turned to the Spoogies. 'You saw
that!' he cried. 'He cheated!'

There was no response.

'Your leader is a fraud,' I said. 'Just as I
promised, I have proved myself the stronger.'

I could sense a great struggle going on in

the minds of the crowd. Then there was a single shout of *Hail!* almost immediately followed by many more cries of *Hail, great one!*

'Listen, I'm just Jams, OK?' I said.

'Hail, Jams the Just!' cried the crowd.

'Stop it! I'm *just* Jams!'

'Teach us to be just, like thee!' cried the crowd.

Suddenly, there was a great kerfuffle. A woman was making her way through the assembled throng.

A woman just like...

'Mum!' I cried.

'Jams!' cried Mum.

We fell into a lovely, loving hug. It was like sinking into a river of warm kittens.

'Who are all these people?' asked Mum.

'They're ... err ... well, I suppose they're my followers, Mum.'

'Hail, Jams' Mum!' someone cried.

'Can you tell them to go away?' asked Mum.

'Err ... I said, 'no offence, but verily I say unto ye, hop it.'

So it was that the siege of Dawson Castle was finally lifted, and great joy was felt by its inhabitants.

Needless to say, Mum was mightily relieved to see Thimble; and Thimble was no less relieved to see Mum. Dad didn't get such a warm welcome, seeing as he was the one who threatened to sell Thimble, but I defended him. I said the thought of seventy-seven thousand pounds would turn anybody's head, especially given the eye-watering debts we'd racked up while Mum was away relaxing.

As usual, I'd said too much.

'I think you've got some explaining to do,' said Mum.

So it was that we explained to Mum about the ill-fated trip to the supermarket, the unfortunate incident with the telegraph pole, the long taxi journey to nowhere, the unfortunate incident with Mum's chocolate, Thimble's boo-boo in IKEA, the unfortunate incident with the wheelbarrow, and all the other interesting adventures which had befallen us. To her credit, Mum took them all in her stride, laughing at all the dumb things that Thimble had done and frowning at all the dumb things done by Dad. The tattoo was the only real problem, until we'd convinced Mum that bananas really meant bananas, and wasn't the nickname of a woman Dad had met while Mum was away.

'I'll get "I Love Nora" next time,' said Dad.

'That's very sweet of you,' said Mum, giving him a little kiss. 'I'm sorry you didn't get to be top of the bestseller charts. By the way, I really should have mentioned, there's a spare key to the petty-cash box taped to the bottom of it.'

'What?' I said.

'I'd rather you hadn't told us that,' said Dad.

'We'll see what's in it and get us a nice takeaway,' said Mum.

'Wicked!' I cried, and Thimble was obviously pleased as well, as he made the sign for 'takeaway' twenty-seven times. I gave him a huge hug.

He may not have been Bob Special, but he sure was special to me.

Other books in this series:

Praise for *Thimble Monkey Superstar*

'An absolutely hilarious story, deservedly shortlisted for the Lollies, Laugh Out Loud Book Awards. This is an imaginative tale,with sharp one liners and a truly batty adventure which is still making me giggle!'
Zoe James-Williams, South Wales Evening Post

'Madcap humour, corny one-liners and ludicrous situations abound in this light-hearted chapter book… The illustrations are suitably wild and wacky and the short, snappy text make this an accessible and fast-paced adventure.'
BookTrust

'It's very funny and the text positively bristles with jokes and snappy one-liners, the butt of most of them being Jams' hapless dad. Nicely divided into satisfying chapters and full of Martin Chatterton's wonderful bug-eyed illustrations, this is easy and addictive reading.' *Andrea Reece, Lovereading4kids*

'A charming and funny book. We really enjoyed the exploits of the mischievous and fiendishly clever monkey.'
Toppsta review

'This book is a must.'
Toppsta review

'A funny, delightful book.'
Boyd Clack

'It was really refreshing to have a main character with a disability – doesn't happen very often. I think it's a great book for all children!'
Toppsta review

'Jams is awesome – he's smart, he's strong and he's funny. We loved Thimble – my son has told me he would love to have a pet monkey too!'
Toppsta review

'*Thimble Monkey Superstar* is hilarious ... this is a truly engaging book, full of hilarious slapstick episodes which invariably end with egg on Dad's face.'
Family Bookworms

THIMBLE MONKEY SUPERSTAR

by Jon Blake, illustrated by Martin Chatterton

SHORTLISTED FOR THE
**LOLLIES LAUGH OUT LOUD
AWARDS 2017**

Selected for the
Summer Reading Challenge 2017
and **Toppsta Summer Reading
Guide 2017**

- **Firefly Press 2016**

- **£5.99**

- **ISBN:
978-1-910080-34-4**

THIMBLE HOLIDAY HAVOC

by Jon Blake, illustrated by Martin Chatterton

When **Mum** organises a house-swap **holiday** to
France, what could possibly **go wrong?** Then
Thimble, **Jams** and **Dad** find the keys to a
speedboat, a **drill** and a makeshift **burglar outfit**
and the adventures really begin.

- **Firefly Press 2018**

  - **£5.99**

  - **ISBN:**
978-191-0080-66-5